BIGMAMA

Harbor
Donald Crews

MULBERRY BOOKS · New York

including
photocopying,
recording or by any
information storage
and retrieval system,
without permission
in writing from
the Publisher,
HarperCollins
Children's Books,
a division of
HarperCollins
Publishers,
10 East 53rd Street,
New York, NY 10022.

Manufactured in China.

13 SCP 20 19 18
17 16 15 14 13

Library of Congress
Cataloging in
Publication Data

Crews, Donald. Harbor.
Summary: Presents
various kinds of
boats which come and
go in a busy harbor.
1. Ships—Pictorial
works—Juvenile
literature.
[1. Harbors. 2. Boats] I. Title.
VM307.C8   623.8′2′00222   81-6607
ISBN 0-688-07332-8

First Mulberry Edition, 1987

To the women in my life
& Malcolm

A harbor.

Wharves, docks, piers, and warehouses.

A port for ships, boats, and cargo.

**Ferryboats shuttle back and forth
from shore to shore.
They do not need to turn around.
The back becomes the front.**

Liners, tankers, tugboats, barges, and freighters move in and out.

**Big boats,
little boats,**

long, low-lying barges,

fast police boats, and
slow-moving lighters
crowd the water.

The tugboat is the busiest boat in the harbor.

**Tugs push.
Tugs tow.**

**Tugs guide big boats
to their docks**

and out again.

**In the harbor the fireboat
is ready for an emergency**

or a celebration.

Ship Shapes

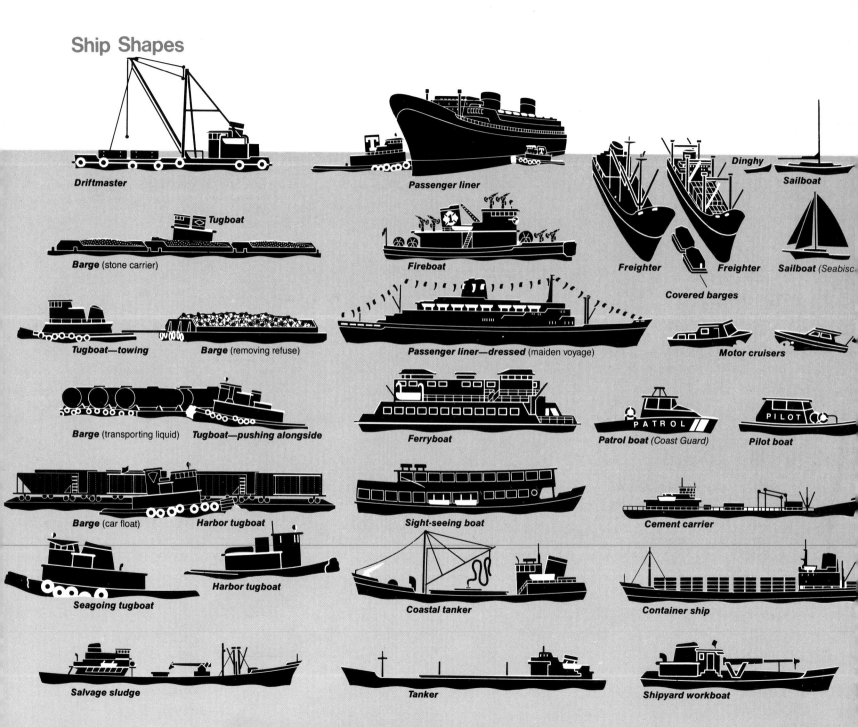

Driftmaster

Passenger liner

Dinghy

Sailboat

Barge (stone carrier)

Tugboat

Fireboat

Freighter

Freighter

Sailboat (Seabisc.

Covered barges

Tugboat—towing

Barge (removing refuse)

Passenger liner—dressed (maiden voyage)

Motor cruisers

Barge (transporting liquid)

Tugboat—pushing alongside

Ferryboat

Patrol boat (Coast Guard)

Pilot boat

Barge (car float)

Harbor tugboat

Sight-seeing boat

Cement carrier

Seagoing tugboat

Harbor tugboat

Coastal tanker

Container ship

Salvage sludge

Tanker

Shipyard workboat